DESTINATION
NORFOLK

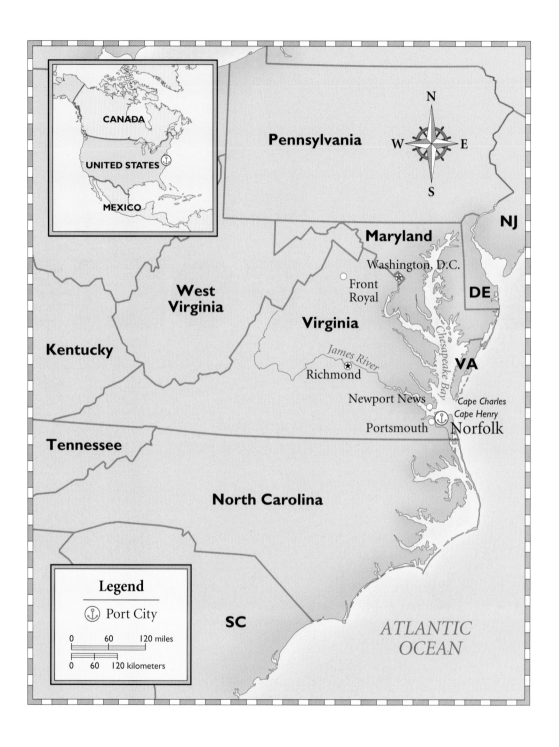

DESTINATION NORFOLK

by Linda Wirkner

Lerner Publications Company · Minneapolis

PHOTO ACKNOWLEDGMENTS

Cover photo by Richard T. Nowitz. All inside photos courtesy of: Hampton Roads Maritime Association: (© Thomas Daniel) pp. 5, 73, (© Jack Will) p. 8, (© Backus Aerial Photography, Inc.) p. 18; Visuals Unlimited: (© Rodney Todt) p. 6, (© P. Slattery) p. 27, (© Audrey Gibson) pp. 62, 66 (bottom); © William B. Folsom, pp. 11, 23; Hampton Roads Maritime Assoc., pp. 14 (top), 48; Virginia Port Authority, pp. 14 (bottom), 19, 21, 22, 54 (top); Virginia International Terminals, pp. 15, 54 (bottom), 56, 61; Cargill, Inc., pp. 17 (top), 53; Norfolk Southern Corp., p. 17; © Ernest H. Robl, pp. 22-23, 51 (both), 52, 66 (top), 69, 71, 75, 76; Fleet and Industrial Supply Center, p. 24; U.S. Army Corps of Engineers, p. 26; America 1585/ © Trustees of the British Museum, British Museum Press, pp. 28, 30; The Library of Virginia, pp. 32, 40, 41, 42; Corbis-Bettmann, p. 33; Norfolk Dept. of Surveys, 35 (inset); Library of Congress, pp. 35, 39 (top); Virginia Historical Society, p. 37; National Archives, p. 39 (bottom); Norfolk Public Library, pp. 43, 46; UPI/Corbis-Bettmann, p. 44; Jim Sutliff/Norfolk Southern Corp., p. 47; Reuters/Mike Theiler/Archive Photos, p. 60; Virginia Tourism Corp., p. 64; © Richard T. Nowitz, p. 72. Maps by Ortelius Design.

For Edith Matotek, in loving memory.

Website address:www.lernerbooks.com

LIBRARY OF CONGRESS CATALOGING-IN-PUBLICATION DATA

Wirkner, Linda
    Destination Norfolk / by Linda Wirkner.
       p. cm. — (Port cities of North America)
    Includes index.
    Summary: An introduction to the port city of Norfolk, Virginia, describing its geography, history, economy, and day-to-day life.
    ISBN 0-8225-2789-8 (lib. bdg. : alk. paper)
    1. Norfolk (Va.)—Juvenile Literature. [1. Norfolk (Va)]
I. Title. II. Series.
F234.N8W77 1998
917.55'521—dc21   96–52013

Manufactured in the United States of America
1 2 3 4 5 6 – JR – 03 02 01 00 99 98

The glossary that begins on page 76 gives definitions of words shown in **bold type** in the text.

CONTENTS

CHAPTER ONE

LAY OF THE LAND

As the early morning sun hangs just above the eastern horizon, a cargo ship advances slowly between two points of land in Virginia known as the Virginia Capes. With Cape Henry to the south and Cape Charles to the north, the mammoth ship passes from the Atlantic Ocean into the Chesapeake Bay—a large saltwater bay on the East Coast of the United States. The tunnel section of the Chesapeake Bay Bridge-Tunnel, a 23-mile-long structure that connects Virginia's mainland with the Eastern Shore Peninsula, lies 90 feet beneath the water. This bridge-tunnel, which travels over and under the Chesapeake Bay, allows automobiles to cross the bay without interfering with shipping activity. The large amount of shipping traffic and the extensive

Sea Gull Island (facing page) *on the Chesapeake Bay Bridge-Tunnel offers onlookers a great view of an incoming tanker.*

network of waterways make underwater tunnels a necessary part of the area's transportation system.

The vessel continues on its path, maneuvering into Hampton Roads. This harbor is formed by the joining of three tidal rivers—the James, the Nansemond, and the Elizabeth. Hampton Roads covers an area of 35 square miles and serves as the approach to the ports of Norfolk, Newport News, and Portsmouth. These three Virginia ports are known collectively as the Port of Hampton Roads. More than 51 million tons of cargo pass through the Port of Hampton Roads each year, and more than 2,500 vessels visit the port annually.

Downtown Norfolk lies on the shores of Hampton Roads, one of the world's finest natural deepwater harbors.

After the cargo ship enters Hampton Roads, it travels over another underwater tunnel—the Hampton Roads Bridge-Tunnel. The ship then turns east into the Elizabeth River, where it follows the 19.5-mile Norfolk Channel. The channel ranges between 45 and 50 feet in depth, ensuring that large oceangoing vessels can move in and out of the harbor with ease. Eighteen miles from the open sea, the freighter has reached its destination—the port city of Norfolk.

Location ➤ Covering 66 square miles in southeastern Virginia, Norfolk is the state's second largest city. Located in the middle of the Atlantic Coast, Virginia is bordered on the northeast by the District of Columbia and Maryland and on the west by Kentucky and West Virginia. North Carolina and Tennessee lie to the south. The Chesapeake Bay forms Norfolk's northern border, while Hampton Roads sits to the west. To the city's east is the Atlantic Ocean. Although port facilities exist throughout the area, Norfolk is the hub of the Port of Hampton Roads. In addition to being a large commercial port, it is also the home of Norfolk Naval Base, a major U.S. naval facility and the world's largest naval installation.

Norfolk is one of the ten busiest ports in the United States, ideally situated midway along the Atlantic Coast of the United States. Because of its central location, Hampton Roads enjoys mild weather and is ice free throughout the year. January is the coldest month with an average daily high temperature of 48°F and an average daily low of 32°F. In July, the hottest

➤ Norfolk Channel is mile zero for the 1,095-mile Atlantic Intracoastal Waterway. The protected inland waterway makes it possible for pleasure boats and commercial ships to travel from Norfolk all the way to Miami, Florida.

➤ The Chesapeake Bay Bridge-Tunnel crosses 17.6 miles of open water and is considered the world's largest bridge-tunnel complex.

month, the average daily high temperature is 87°F, and the average daily low is 70°F. The mild climate attracts shipping lines and contributes to the port's continued growth.

The port's location also plays a major role in attracting commercial traffic. Ships can leave the docks and reach open ocean in less than three hours. Shipping lines, which may spend more than $40,000 each day to operate just one ship, like the easy access to the ocean because it cuts down on travel time to and from markets and saves money. As a result, the Port of Hampton Roads draws more than 75 shipping lines from Europe, the Middle East, Africa, Asia, South America, Australia, and the Caribbean.

The natural depth of Hampton Roads allows the port to accommodate large vessels. Two natural deep-draft anchorages are located near the entrance to the harbor. These anchorages, which serve as holding areas for ships waiting to unload their cargoes, can fit about 120 vessels at one time. In addition, four anchorages have been dredged (cleared) in the inner harbor to accommodate up to 40 more vessels. **Dredging** is required at the port because the James, Nansemond, and Elizabeth Rivers all deposit silt into the inner harbor. Without dredging, the buildup of silt would prevent large ships from navigating harbor waters.

The Virginia Pilot Association provides pilots for large cargo ships coming into the port. Pilots are local experts who guide freighters through the Norfolk Channel and on to various port facilities. As a cargo ship approaches Hampton Roads, the captain makes radio contact to identify the vessel and its location and

The port's channels must be dredged to accommodate tankers and other large cargo vessels.

to request the assistance of a pilot. A pilots' station—located at Chesapeake Bay Buoy J, just off Cape Henry—serves as the point where pilots take over. Special traffic lanes designated by standard maritime buoys mark the main shipping channel. By following these buoys, ships avoid areas where the channel may be relatively shallow. Pilots also have to be aware of shipwrecks, reefs, rock formations, and oyster fishing areas. The U.S. Coast Guard Marine Safety Office helps control vessel movement within the port by maintaining a daily list of merchant vessel arrivals.

Port Facilities ▶ The port facilities at Norfolk handle large volumes of nearly every type of cargo. The coal, grain, and fertilizers that pass through Norfolk are examples of dry **bulk cargo,** which is raw material loaded loosely on board ships.

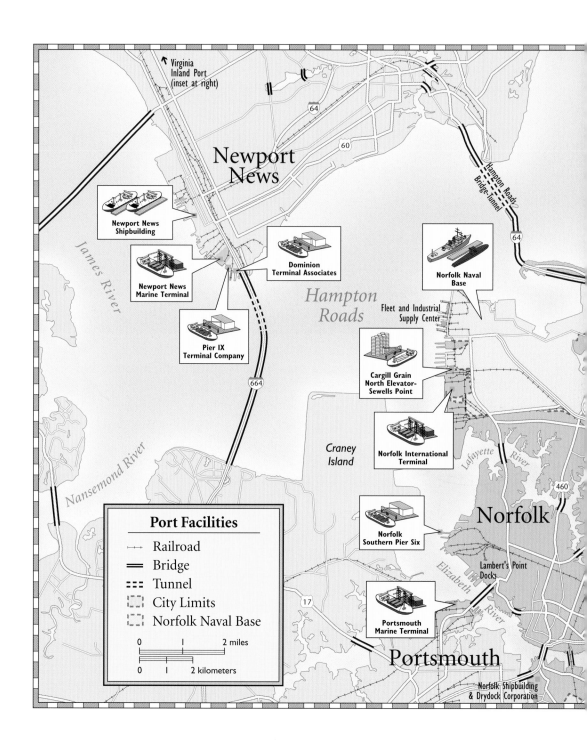

Virginia
Inland Port
(inset at right)

64

60

Newport News

Hampton Roads Bridge-tunnel

64

Newport News Shipbuilding

Newport News Marine Terminal

Dominion Terminal Associates

Hampton Roads

Norfolk Naval Base

Fleet and Industrial Supply Center

James River

Pier IX Terminal Company

Cargill Grain North Elevator-Sewells Point

664

Lafayette River

Craney Island

Norfolk International Terminal

460

Nansemond River

Norfolk

Port Facilities

↦ Railroad
━ Bridge
┅ Tunnel
▢ City Limits
▢ Norfolk Naval Base

0	1	2 miles

0	1	2 kilometers

Norfolk Southern Pier Six

Lambert's Point Docks

Elizabeth River

17

Portsmouth Marine Terminal

Portsmouth

Norfolk Shipbuilding & Drydock Corporation

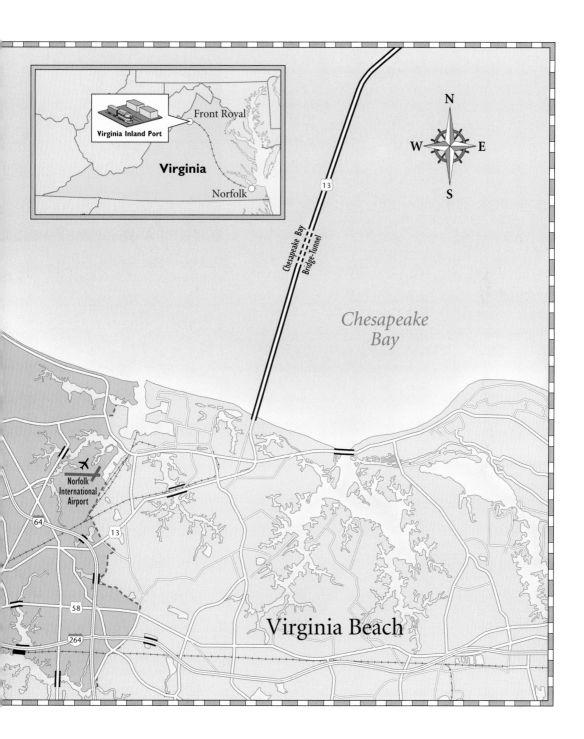

Front Royal

Virginia Inland Port

Virginia

Norfolk

13

Chesapeake Bay Bridge-Tunnel

N

W   E

S

Chesapeake Bay

Norfolk International Airport

64

13

58

264

Virginia Beach

Norfolk also handles liquid bulk cargoes, such as oil. **Breakbulk cargo**—which is shipped in separate units such as boxes or pallets—includes rubber, cacao beans (from which chocolate is made), automobiles, and heavy machinery. Some products arrive at the port in containers. These large, metal, reusable boxes protect cargo from weather and vandalism and ensure safe handling. Container cargo at Norfolk includes paper products, textile yarns, plastics, poultry, and auto parts.

Spreading across 811 acres, Norfolk International Terminal (NIT) is the largest terminal within the Port of Hampton Roads. With a wide range of facilities, NIT can handle a variety of import and export cargo. Equipment on each of the terminal's three main concrete piers includes forklifts of all sizes, tractors, and **gantry cranes.** The terminal's four container berths are equipped with mechanical handling facilities that include three Kone dual-hoist

A port worker guides breakbulk cargo off a ship.

At Norfolk International Terminal, a loaded container ship heads for a berthing space.

After a container ship has docked, gantry crane operators direct the movement of the crane along the vessel to unload the cargo.

> ➤ Kone dual-hoist cranes are the largest and fastest in the country. Port engineers designed these cranes, which can handle 50 percent more containers than the industry average.

hydraulic cranes, a special type of gantry crane used to move containers. These cranes go through a series of automatic adjustments to prevent containers from swaying back and forth as they are being lifted on and off ships. With the sway eliminated, containers can be lifted more quickly and safely. In addition, these towering orange giants have doubled NIT's handling capacity from about 25 containers an hour to 50 containers an hour. The terminal can store approximately 30,000 **TEUs** (20-foot equivalent units—the size of a standard shipping container).

Breakbulk cargo is unloaded at Piers One, Two, and Three. The covered, concrete space at these piers can accommodate up to eight ships at a time. Eight brick and concrete warehouses, divided by fire walls into smaller compartments, provide storage space. The warehouses offer dry storage areas as well as cold storage for perishable cargo such as meat. In addition, NIT has a 900-foot berth for roll-on/roll-off vessels. Ro-ro ships are equipped with ramps so that automobiles, off-road construction equipment, and containers mounted on wheels can drive directly on and off the ships.

Besides the three piers at NIT, other port facilities within the city include the piers at Lambert's Point, which are owned and operated by Lambert's Point Docks, Inc. These piers work together as a general marine terminal and transit warehouse operation, handling and storing a variety of goods. The pier facilities provide space for berthing six vessels at a time, with two berths for ro-ro ships. Eight adjacent warehouses offer one million square feet of storage space. A fumigation facility is available for spraying restricted imports, such as cotton or secondhand bagging, that may carry pests.

Two terminals in Norfolk deal specifically with dry bulk cargo. At Norfolk Southern Pier Six, the Norfolk Southern Corporation oversees the fastest coal-handling facility in the world. The pier has two traveling loaders, each one as high as a 17-story building, that can work on two ships at once or can concentrate on a single collier (coal ship). When both loaders work on a single ship, up to 150,000 tons of coal can be loaded or unloaded in an hour. In addition to the loading pier, Norfolk Southern also handles coal weighing, thawing, sampling, and

➤ The fumigation plant at NIT can hold up 228 hogsheads of tobacco. A hogshead is a barrel-like container that holds 8.42 cubic feet. NIT also houses a defrost plant for the inspection of imported meat.

➤ Both U.S. Customs and the Department of Agriculture maintain offices at NIT with services available 24 hours a day.

dumping facilities. Located at Sewells Point is a grain-loading facility—operated by Cargill, Inc.—that moves barley, wheat, soybeans, and corn. The wharf at Sewells Point extends 1,035 feet and has three fully automated ship loaders. Ships can be filled at rates of up to 50,000 bushels per hour. The grain elevator at the facility has a storage capacity of three million bushels.

Norfolk provides shipping companies with a number of port-related services. Warehouses in Norfolk offer storage and distribution services for importers and exporters. The port's **dry docks** lift vessels completely out of the water for repairs. Tugboats and towing services help large cargo ships dock and undock, while ship **chandlers** provide vessels with food and supplies. In addition, the Norfolk Seamen's Friend Society operates a recreation center for American and international sailors.

Cargill, Inc., a major grain distributor, runs grain-loading facilities in Norfolk and in Chesapeake (above). *At Norfolk Southern Pier Six* (right), *a traveling loader dumps coal into the cargo holds of a dry bulk tanker.*

The port facilities in Newport News and Portsmouth also play an important role in shipping activity. Located in Newport News on the east bank of the James River are two large coal-handling terminals run by Pier IX Terminal Company and Dominion Terminal Associates. Next to these facilities is Newport News Marine Terminal, which handles steel products, locomotive engines, and automobiles. Newport

The port's reliable fleet of tugboats perform many tasks, including moving heavy gantry cranes.

News is also the home of Newport News Shipbuilding, where skilled workers design, construct, and repair a variety of ships. Portsmouth Marine Terminal is the second largest container terminal within the Port of Hampton Roads, and it also handles ro-ro cargo. Portsmouth Marine Terminal and Newport News Marine Terminal work in conjunction with NIT, under the management of the Virginia Port Authority.

A flatbed truck waits to be loaded with containers at Newport News Marine Terminal. Containers are designed to ride on truck trailers and railroad flatcars.

Transportation Networks ▶ Three different railroads serve Norfolk's port facilities. Norfolk Southern's 14,500-mile network connects the port to 20 states in the southeastern and midwestern United States, as well as to Ontario, Canada. This railroad manages a large volume of the export cargo that moves through Norfolk and represents an important link to major midwestern cities such as Chicago, Detroit, and Cincinnati. CSX, another railway company, has approximately 21,000 miles of track that connect 22 states and Canada to Norfolk's port facilities. Norfolk &

Portsmouth Belt Line Railroad hooks up with all rail lines entering Norfolk and serves a large number of manufacturing industries located away from the waterfront.

More than 135 trucking companies also operate in the area of the port. Trucks have immediate access to Interstate 64, which runs east and west and connects to Interstate 95, which runs north and south. These interstate highways—along with an efficient network of local highways, tunnels, and bridges—allow trucking services to link the port with the rest of the country. Air services are also readily available for transporting cargo after it has arrived by ship. Norfolk International Airport operates two air cargo terminals that handle nearly 46 million pounds of cargo annually. Air freight includes everything from massive industrial machinery to perfume and fresh seafood.

Although many of the port's facilities are fully ◀ **Port Operations** automated and are designed for high-speed cargo transfer, dockworkers play an important role in the efficient operation of the port. Longshoremen oversee the physical loading and discharging of cargo on and off vessels. Other dockworkers, called shortshoremen, take care of checking, moving, packing, and crating cargo at the terminals.

Many of the manufactured goods that come into the port are packed in containers. Huge cranes transfer the containers from ships and stack them onto trains or trucks for the trip to market. Dockside rail service at NIT and other terminals simplifies this system of **inter-modal transportation,** by which cargo moves from one type of vehicle to another in the course of a single trip. Railroad tracks feed directly into warehouses and alongside docked ships to allow for convenient transfer of containers. As a result, products can be shipped to market quickly and efficiently.

An important intermodal link to the Port of Hampton Roads is the Virginia Inland Port in Front Royal, Virginia, which serves as a container transfer facility. Trucks transport containers to Front Royal, where they are loaded onto trains headed for port terminals in Hampton Roads or for markets in northern Virginia, West Virginia, Maryland, Pennsylvania, and eastern Ohio.

The Port of Hampton Roads has 30 miles of dockside rail, which enables port workers to transfer cargo directly from ships to trains.

New technology at the Hampton Roads ports has helped improve cargo transfer. The Synchronous Planning and Real Time Control System, known as SPARCS, manages the movement of cargo through terminals and gate complexes and is used in yard management, gate assignment, vessel stowage, and rail planning.

Yard management involves determining the exact position for every move of cargo or equipment. The gate-assignment feature receives information from the yard-management module, which tells truck drivers at the gate exactly where to go in the yard to either pick up or drop off a container. The vessel-stowage system plans exactly how cargo should be arranged on ships and sets up a logical order in which to stow the containers efficiently. The rail-planning feature helps operators transfer containers between ships and railroad cars. As cargo enters and exits the terminals, workers update SPARCS using hand-held computers. Tracking cargo in this way not only enables goods to be moved more efficiently, it also allows shipping customers to find out the status and location of their cargo at any time.

Using hand-held computers, workers at the port can easily track the movement of cargo.

Norfolk Naval Base is home to a variety of U.S. military vessels, including submarines (above) *and destroyers* (right).

Norfolk Naval Base ➤ Located in the Sewells Point area of Norfolk is Norfolk Naval Base, the home port for more than 100 U.S. Navy vessels. When these ships are not at sea, they are docked at the base's 15 piers for repair and refit. Port facilities at the base extend more than four miles and include seven miles of berthing space. Port services control the arrival and departure of more than 3,100 ships annually. The huge Fleet and

The Fleet and Industrial Supply Center (FISC), the U.S. Navy's largest field supply operation, contains more than 8 million square feet of storage space. FISC provides ships with everything from oil to household items.

Industrial Supply Center (FISC), located across from Piers Three and Four, provides logistics and support to naval operations around the world. FISC manages stock of more than 600,000 types of supplies and ships these supplies to naval vessels in the Atlantic Ocean, the Mediterranean Sea, the Indian Ocean, and the Persian Gulf.

Away from the port, Norfolk Naval Base houses the headquarters of the U.S. Atlantic Fleet, which is responsible for the defense of the entire Atlantic Ocean—from the North Pole to the South Pole and from the eastern United States to the western coast of Africa. The base is also the headquarters for the North Atlantic

➤ Norfolk Naval Base occupies more than 25 percent of the land in Norfolk and employs more people than any other naval base in the United States.

Treaty Organization (NATO) Supreme Allied Command Atlantic. This command is responsible for all land, air, and sea operations carried out by NATO forces.

Ballast Dumping ➤
Causes Problems

> ➤ The Port of Hampton Roads and the nearby Port of Baltimore are both on the Chesapeake Bay. They receive a combined three billion gallons of ballast water annually, more than any other area along the Atlantic Coast.

At ports all over the world, ships empty their **ballast tanks** in harbor waters. The dumping and taking on of ballast is a necessary part of operating a large cargo vessel. As ships travel from port to port unloading or loading cargo, they take in or release extra water to remain stable. Ballast dumping is a problem for Norfolk and other Hampton Roads ports. Ballast tanks of giant freight ships frequently contain algae, fish, worms, and crabs. Often these species aren't native to the Chesapeake Bay and can force out or kill off local marine species. Some refer to this occurrence as biological pollution.

A large ship's ballast tanks can hold millions of gallons of water. Thousands of different organisms may be swimming around in the tanks. Some may be microscopic bacteria that pose health threats to humans. Others may be algae that cause red tides, a reddish discoloration of seawater. Some red tides are harmless, but others can be highly toxic to a variety of animals. Clams, oysters, and other shellfish feed on these organisms and concentrate the poisons in their bodies. Humans or other animals who eat the contaminated shellfish may suffer paralysis or even death.

Scientists believe that the number of species invading U.S. waters has been increasing in recent years as world trade has grown. And ships have become faster, creating the likelihood that organisms in ballast tanks will survive the trip

Ballast dumping and red tides can greatly damage Norfolk's marine environment, depriving fish and other sea creatures of a healthy habitat.

to port. The large amount of shipping activity in the Chesapeake Bay makes the area prone to biological pollution. To stem the potential danger, the U.S. Coast Guard has called for a voluntary program to encourage ships to exchange their ballast water out in the Atlantic Ocean before entering the Chesapeake Bay. Species picked up in harbors that have a low concentration of salt would die when released into the ocean's highly salty water. And any organisms sucked into ballast tanks along with ocean water are less likely to survive if released in the Chesapeake Bay.

Although voluntary, this program will help Norfolk become more environmentally friendly while still maintaining its status as one of the busiest U.S. ports. The health of the Chesapeake Bay and Hampton Roads is important for everyone who lives and works in Norfolk. With a bustling port and a healthy environment, Norfolk will continue to be the hub of the Virginia waterfront.

CRANEY ISLAND

Dredging channels and harbors to keep waters deep enough to accommodate large ships creates large volumes of dredged materials that must be disposed of safely. The Port of Hampton Roads resolved this problem with the creation of a 2,500-acre disposal area on Craney Island. The U.S. Corps of Engineers manages the site. Craney Island provides a low cost, environmentally favorable site for depositing dredged material.

Besides holding dredged material, Craney Island also provides a habitat (home) for more than 150 species of birds. Reeds and grasses that grow on dredged soil make an ideal nesting ground for these birds. A bird protection program—run jointly by the College of William and Mary and the Department of Game and Inland Fisheries—has resulted in the increased population of the piping plover and the least tern, two common coastal species.

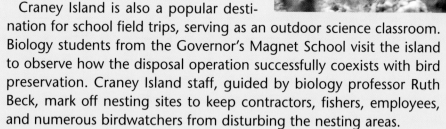

Craney Island is also a popular destination for school field trips, serving as an outdoor science classroom. Biology students from the Governor's Magnet School visit the island to observe how the disposal operation successfully coexists with bird preservation. Craney Island staff, guided by biology professor Ruth Beck, mark off nesting sites to keep contractors, fishers, employees, and numerous birdwatchers from disturbing the nesting areas.

In recognition of their efforts, the staff at Craney Island Dredged Material Area received the Virginia Society of Ornithology Jack M. Abbott Conservation Award for 1996. On Craney Island, people and nature manage to live side by side.

CHAPTER TWO

A HISTORIC SOUTHERN PORT

Native American Traders ▶ Long before European explorers first sailed into the Chesapeake Bay, many Native American peoples inhabited the area. These groups included the Chesapeake, the Chickahominy, the Kiskiack, the Kecoughtan, and the Nansemond. Linked by similar customs and closely related Algonquian languages, these groups are often referred to as Algonquian peoples. The Algonquian nations inhabited a vast region that included the present-day Great Lakes, southeastern Canada, New England, and the mid-Atlantic states. The groups lived by hunting, fishing, gathering, and farming. Around the

A number of Algonquian-speaking Native groups lived in the coastal lowlands along the Chesapeake Bay and the Atlantic Coast. Native villages consisted of houses built with bent saplings, tree bark, and marsh plants.

Dugout canoes, some stretching as long as 50 feet, were an important form of transportation for Native peoples living along the coast.

Chesapeake Bay, hunters tracked a variety of game, including deer, beavers, and otters. Fishers used spears and nets to gather their catches in the area's rivers and bays. Algonquian farmers also grew crops such as corn and pumpkins.

The extensive waterways of the coastal region provided Native peoples with ample opportunity for trade. They carried their goods in canoes, cruising tidal rivers that reach more than 100 miles inland. Native traders also journeyed across the Chesapeake Bay, which cuts inland more than 200 miles. Using large canoes that held 30 or 40 people, coastal peoples living on the west side of the Chesapeake Bay crossed the

➤ Shell beads, called wampum, were used for ceremony as well as trade. Wampum belts detailed tribal records and communicated messages of war and peace to other groups. When Indians began trading with the British, wampum became a form of money.

➤ Archaeologists have dug up shells and shell beads from the Atlantic Coast in many parts of Virginia. Their findings are a good indication that coastal Indians traded with Indians living farther inland.

wide expanse of water to trade copper, skins, and shell beads with groups on the eastern shore. Coastal peoples also traded with the Tockwogh Indians, who lived at the head of the bay. From the Tockwogh Indians they received iron goods. The Tockwogh obtained these iron goods from inland Susquehannock Indians, who lived along the Susquehanna River that runs through modern-day New York, Pennsylvania, and Maryland.

In addition to using the area's extensive waterways, coastal Indian groups traveled inland following trails first made by grazing animals. Years later the first wagons widened these trails. The trails gradually became roads and eventually were turned into Virginia's modern highways.

European Explorers ➤ In the early 1500s, Spanish explorers looking for a route to Asia became the first Europeans to visit the Chesapeake Bay area. They hoped the bay would lead inland to a passage that would connect to the Pacific Ocean. In 1561 another Spanish expedition sailed into the lower Chesapeake Bay. Kiskiack Indians offered furs and fresh provisions to the crew in return for copper vessels and iron axes. Hoping to convert the Native peoples to Christianity, the Spanish built several missions along the Bay and the James River.

Early Spanish explorers returned to Europe with tales of finding gold, silver, and other riches in North America. As a result, England and other European countries became interested in exploring and settling the continent. James I, king of England (James VI of Scotland), formed the Virginia Charter Company to establish a colony that would bring Christianity to the region's Native peoples and would provide a new market for the kingdoms' manufactured goods.

In 1607 the Virginia Charter Company sent a group of 105 settlers across the Atlantic Ocean in three ships. The vessels ventured into the Chesapeake Bay and landed at Cape Henry. The group then sailed up the James River and settled on a peninsula, which they named Jamestown, after the king. The settlement lay in the territory of a confederacy of more than 30 Indian groups, headed by Chief Powhatan. Captain John Smith, who led the settlement party, immediately visited with the Powhatan Indians to set up trade.

> ➤ Chief Powhatan's Algonquian name was Wahunsonacock. The colonists had trouble pronouncing his name, so they started calling him by his tribal name.

Trade with Native peoples helped the Jamestown colonists survive the first few difficult years. The distrust the two groups had for one another, however, eventually led to bloodshed.

As the tobacco trade grew, British tobacco ships became a common sight along the James River.

The Jamestown colony relied on trade with Indians out of necessity. Disease and starvation killed many of the early settlers, who had come to search for treasure but were not prepared to work for their survival. Through trade the colonists received corn, while the Indians obtained British goods such as glass beads, iron and copper bracelets, and kettles. Trade between the groups was also a foundation for a tentative peace.

When the next ship of British settlers arrived at Jamestown several months later, Chief Powhatan discovered that the new arrivals were willing to trade three or four times more than Smith's colonists had offered for corn. Powhatan began asking Captain Smith for the higher amount. Chief Powhatan and Captain Smith finally came to a compromise. Powhatan agreed to accept two or three pounds of blue beads in exchange for two or three bushels of corn. This was probably one of the earliest documented examples of trade negotiating in North America.

Jamestown colonist John Rolfe discovered a crop that would later become Virginia's prize trade item. In 1613, after much experimenting, he developed a variety of tobacco that became very popular with people in Britain. Tobacco proved to be an ideal trading commodity. If cured properly, it held up well in transit and brought a good price. Because the shipping weight was low, it was also a profitable cargo to ship. By 1618 the colony was sending 50,000 pounds of tobacco to Britain each year. By 1628 the annual amount of tobacco bound for Britain was more than 500,000 pounds. In return for a small amount of tobacco, a Virginia farmer could receive clothing for six people, two guns, ammunition, assorted tools, and other useful goods. The farmer could keep these items or trade them for livestock, land, or whatever else was needed.

Growing tobacco for trade proved to be an excellent way for the colonists to survive and prosper. However, as the tobacco trade prospered and as more settlers arrived from Britain, relations with Native peoples deteriorated. Farmers needed more land to grow tobacco, and they pushed the Indians of the area farther west. In addition, the largest tobacco estates, or plantations, began importing captured Africans to use as a slave labor force.

◄ **Birth of a Port City**

In 1680 the Virginia General Assembly founded a port in Norfolk County to serve ships carrying tobacco to and from Britain. Norfolk was created to be a central point for the shipment of tobacco and for the collection of revenues for the British crown. In 1691 the General Assembly passed the Act for Establishing Ports and Markets, which named Norfolk and 16 other Virginia towns as ports. Soon trade from the Port of Norfolk extended to Britain, the Caribbean, and Africa. Norfolk also traded wool, leather, cattle, hogs, and pine tar with neighboring British colonies in New England.

In 1761 the Virginia colony appointed a group of trustees to build a wharf and to make other improvements to the Port of Norfolk. As a result of this expansion, Norfolk soon became the principal military and commercial seaport of Virginia. The port was deep enough for a 40-gun ship and had every kind of convenience

Captains of British ships did not like navigating Virginia's shallow inland waterways. In response, colonial legislators organized the construction of towns, such as Norfolk, (above) *where tobacco ships could be loaded for the overseas journey. This reproduction of an early map* (inset) *shows Norfolk in 1682.*

for loading and unloading large vessels. As Virginia's trade grew, bigger ships were needed to accommodate larger volumes of cargo. Because these larger ships could not navigate Virginia's inland rivers, planters began sending their produce down the James and York Rivers by small craft to Norfolk, where oceangoing vessels took on cargo bound for overseas markets.

Tobacco was still the colony's most profitable export at this time, but the grain trade was steadily growing as well. The increase in grain traffic was the result of crop rotation. Many tobacco growers relied on this farming technique to replace soil nutrients that tobacco crops used up. Farmers replanted tobacco fields with a grain crop, such as corn or wheat, because these grains helped replenish the soil so that fields could later be planted with tobacco. Farmers who relied on crop rotation had large amounts of wheat and corn to sell. At the same time, demand for wheat in the Caribbean, Spain, and Portugal encouraged more wheat production in Virginia, Maryland, and North Carolina. As a result, Norfolk became a center of the grain trade. Norfolk's exports also included pork, candles, tallow, ham, bacon, corn, flour, butter, cheese, lumber, and naval supplies.

While Norfolk was becoming a major port, tension was growing between the colonists and Britain, which ruled Virginia and the 12 other colonies. By the 1770s, more colonists had begun arguing in favor of independence. British restrictions on colonial trade, known as the Navigation Acts, were a major source of discontent. The disagreement grew more heated until war broke out in 1775.

Feeling threatened by the Virginia revolutionists, Lord Dunmore, British governor of the colony, fled the capital city of Williamsburg, Virginia. Dunmore assembled a fleet in Norfolk's waters, and British soldiers briefly occupied the town before being defeated by colonial forces. Hoping to retake the town, Dunmore commanded the British fleet to open fire on Norfolk. The exploding shells caused several fires that quickly spread, but many of the fires were started by colonial soldiers who did not want Norfolk to fall into British hands intact. Most of the town went up in flames.

➤ Incoming ships sometimes brought problems to Norfolk during the 1700s. Crew members on vessels occasionally carried deadly diseases such as smallpox, causing numerous epidemics to spread throughout the city.

➤ By 1761 the British government had passed 29 acts limiting colonial trade. The act of 1660 required that all tobacco from British colonies in North America be transported to Britain, even if the final destination was another country.

Although Lord Dunmore (left) *commanded his forces to fire on Norfolk, much of the town was destroyed by blazes set by colonial soldiers. The rebels publicly blamed the British, turning the destruction into an anti-British propaganda campaign.*

In 1779, when the American Revolution was well underway, the British returned to the area in a surprise attack. They captured large amounts of supplies and vessels and laid waste to the towns of Portsmouth and Suffolk. Hampton Roads endured more destruction than any other area in the colonies. Norfolk's shipping industry didn't recover from wartime damage for several years. However, the colonists' victory in the war did lead to independence, to the establishment of the United States, and to statehood for Virginia.

Norfolk's trade was again seriously hampered during the War of 1812, another confrontation between Britain and the United States. The British blockaded the Chesapeake Bay to keep U.S. ships from entering or leaving the port. But local merchants found ways to get around this blockade. Small ships traveled south through the Dismal Swamp Canal, a waterway connecting the southern branch of the Elizabeth River to the Pasquotank River in North Carolina. The ships carried produce to ports on North Carolina's Albemarle Sound, where the cargo was transferred to smaller vessels that could slip through the blockade and travel to markets in the Caribbean and Europe. These efforts kept many Norfolk traders from declaring bankruptcy.

The arrival of the first steamboat in Norfolk in
1815 allowed produce merchants in Virginia's interior to more easily transport their goods to Norfolk's wharves. Steamboats navigated Virginia's rivers faster than smaller sailing vessels did and provided a means of transport that was preferable to Virginia's rough overland roads. Steam packets, which differed from ordinary trading vessels because they maintained a fixed schedule of service, became popular freight and passenger carriers in Norfolk's waters.

Over the next 40 years, business at the Port of Norfolk declined. British and U.S. trade restrictions cut off Norfolk's merchants from trade with British colonies in the Caribbean. At the same time, the Port of New York was becoming the premier port on the East Coast, commanding a majority of the international trade. Norfolk was a spacious and safe port but not a center of shipping.

When the Civil War between the Northern states and the Southern states erupted in 1861, Norfolk once again suffered. The U.S. Navy blockaded Norfolk and other Southern ports. This action virtually stopped trade, and commerce shriveled. By the end of the war, in 1865, Norfolk's docks were quiet. Yet, as Virginia and other Southern states began to rebuild from wartime damage, port activity increased. Thousands of tradespeople, shipbuilders, laborers, and other workers thronged to the area in search of port-related jobs.

The development of Virginia's railroad network in the 1870s helped revive the Port of Norfolk by providing greater access to inland markets. Norfolk's inadequate rail service had

> ➤ During a yellow fever epidemic in 1855, one third of Norfolk's population died. Yellow Fever Memorial Park, the site of a mass burial for the yellow fever victims, was dedicated in 1993.

been completely destroyed during the war, but newly established railways connected Norfolk to the west and the south with service provided by Norfolk & Western and Seaboard & Roanoke Railroad companies. These railroad lines

The engagement between the **Monitor** *and the* **Merrimac** (right) *in Hampton Roads in 1862 was the first battle between ironclad ships. The destruction caused by the Civil War left the Norfolk Navy Yard* (below) *in ruins.*

Port workers move bales of cotton at a Norfolk warehouse. By 1874 Norfolk was second only to New Orleans in the number of cotton bales handled.

brought lumber, wheat, tobacco, and cotton to Norfolk's wharves. Workers built railroad lines directly to the port, so longshoremen could easily transfer cargo from train to ship.

As a result of railroad expansion, bigger freighters were built to ship larger amounts of cargo. With its deepwater harbor, Norfolk was the only Virginia port that could accommodate these larger vessels. Before long, produce and manufactured goods came to Norfolk by rail from all over Virginia, as well as from other Southern states. In 1881 Norfolk's exports totaled nearly nine times those of Richmond, which had previously been the state's commercial center.

In the 1870s and 1880s, cotton and coal became Norfolk's two largest exports. With the expansion of the railroads, cotton flowed into Norfolk from Georgia, Tennessee, and North Carolina. By 1874 Norfolk ranked second in volume among the country's cotton-exporting ports. Ten years later, nearly half a million bales of cotton per year passed through the port. In 1883 the Norfolk & Western Railroad began

The collier Neptune *fills up with coal at the Norfolk & Western Elevated Coal Pier. Elevators lifted railcars onto the top of the pier, where the cars would dump their cargo into waiting ships.*

shipping millions of tons of coal through Norfolk from newly opened coal fields in Virginia and West Virginia. The ports of Norfolk and Newport News together became the largest coal-exporting ports in the world. By the early 1900s, three major railroads transported coal to Virginia for shipment all over the world.

THE JAMESTOWN EXPOSITION

In 1907 Norfolk hosted the Jamestown Exposition to commemorate the 300-year anniversary of the establishment of Jamestown as the first permanent English settlement in North America. Located on a 367-acre piece of land at Sewells Point, the exposition was a miniature city that included structures devoted to the arts, science, machinery, and transportation, as well as replicas of 21 of the nation's historic statehouses. President Theodore Roosevelt opened the event and launched the Great White Fleet of U.S. Navy ships on its world tour. Thousands of people visited the exposition.

The Jamestown Exposition was a celebration of Norfolk's return to prominence. After the destruction caused by the American Revolution and the Civil War, and the loss of imports to New York and other East Coast ports, Norfolk had been reduced to a minor role in international shipping. The exposition called attention to Norfolk's splendid harbor, to its network of railways, and to the numerous shipping lines carrying cargo in and out of the port. The event was the culmination of 40 years of growth. With the Jamestown Exposition, Norfolk announced to the world that it was once again a major U.S. port.

The growth of the cotton and coal trades established Norfolk as a major U.S. port. Norfolk's export business placed it ahead of ports in Philadelphia, Boston, and Baltimore. Port activity created an enormous number of jobs. Between 1880 and 1910, Norfolk's population tripled as people flocked to the city for work. Newport News Shipbuilding became the state's largest employer, hiring laborers to build and repair vessels.

World Wars ➤ During World War I (1914–1918) and World War II (1939–1945), shipbuilding at Norfolk boomed, and port activity increased. During World War I, established patterns of ship and rail traffic led officials to choose the Norfolk area as the site for the country's largest army supply base, for the headquarters of the U.S. Navy's Atlantic Fleet, and for a new naval base.

Business thrived as a result of the First World War. Guns, food, and war materials from around the country passed through the port for export to war zones in Europe. Coal was the principal export, since the war had created a great need for fuel in Europe. Because of the huge volume of cargo and traffic, railroads and port facilities had to be upgraded. The global conflict also created a need for more ships. Laborers from all over the United States traveled to Newport News to join in the shipbuilding frenzy. By 1917 shipyard employment had jumped to 20 times what it had been in 1915.

With the end of World War I, export traffic at Norfolk dropped quickly. But the total amount of export cargo was still 10 times higher than it had been before the war. Imports rose, but because

Naval recruits take part in maneuvers at St. Helena Training Station. In 1917 the station was moved to Sewells Point and became Norfolk Naval Base.

In the 1940s, workers in Newport News helped the war effort by building battleships such as the USS Indiana, *which saw action in World War II.*

the military no longer needed large numbers of ships, the shipbuilding business plummeted.

When the United States entered World War II in 1941, the Norfolk area experienced yet another shipbuilding boom. Norfolk's piers were busy, shipping troops and military equipment to Europe and North Africa. But coal traffic through the port dropped, as shippers chose to send coal by rail rather than to ship the fuel across the Atlantic Ocean, where vessels risked attack by German U-boats. Toward the end of the war, the U-boat threat lessened, and coal shipments to Europe resumed.

When the war ended in 1945, the boom in Norfolk continued. With the presence of the naval base, Norfolk became a hub of military activity. The civilian population stabilized because many workers remained after their war-related jobs ended. Tourism increased, and retail and service industries expanded to meet the needs of the growing population. Unemployment was low, and incomes were high. In addition, the revival of the postwar European economies created more demand for high-quality coal, so exports went up.

The city of Norfolk, realizing it could not depend solely on the military for its financial stability, looked to the port as a source of income. The city established the Norfolk Port Authority in 1948 to sell shippers on the advantages of the port. In 1952 the Virginia States Port Authority was created to promote the port facilities of Hampton Roads. At this time, railroad companies owned all the piers and could not afford to improve them. The Port Authority proposed that the state buy the piers, make improvements, and lease them back to the railroads to operate. In 1960 the General Assembly approved the purchase.

Growth of the Port > In the mid-1970s, oil suppliers in the Middle East raised the price of oil, creating a global oil

crisis. U.S. coal exports rose as countries all over the world began to substitute coal for oil as a primary fuel. By 1980 Norfolk and other Hampton Roads ports were exporting about 50 million tons of coal each year.

In the early 1980s, labor unrest in Poland disrupted that country's international coal shipments. Suddenly customers from all over the world began depending on Hampton Roads for coal. But when Poland's disputes were resolved, it managed to reclaim its share of the global coal-exporting business. Soon other coal exporters joined the international market. When world oil prices eventually dropped and coal was no longer in such huge demand, Norfolk needed to do something to boost business. The port decided to attract containerized cargo

During the 1970s and early 1980s, the Norfolk Southern coal piers bustled with activity, as global demand for coal rose to new levels.

from other U.S. ports, particularly from nearby Baltimore, Maryland. During the mid-1980s, Norfolk, Portsmouth, and Newport News saw large increases in container traffic.

Before 1982 these three ports had all been owned and operated separately. Efforts to draw new business were splintered, often resulting in intraport competition that hampered growth for all the ports. None of the ports could afford to upgrade equipment or to expand facilities.

In 1982 The Virginia General Assembly passed legislation to unify the ports, creating the Port of Hampton Roads under a common management bureau named the Virginia Port Authority (VPA). A state agency, the VPA is charged with operating and marketing the marine terminal facilities through which shipping trade takes place. These include Norfolk International Terminal (NIT), Portsmouth Marine Terminal, Newport News Marine Terminal, and the Virginia Inland Port in Front Royal. Under VPA management, facilities at all the Hampton Roads terminals have been greatly improved and expanded, and the amount of domestic and international cargo passing through the port has increased.

Working with the other Hampton Roads ports has helped Norfolk maintain its historic status as a leading U.S. port and has provided Norfolk with state-of-the-art equipment. NIT is in the first phase of a 10-year expansion. The plan includes building a new wharf and adding 44 acres of container storage. Doubling Virginia's largest intermodal marine terminal by the year 2010 is the goal of the VPA, as it works to ensure a stronger future.

Upgrading and modernizing port facilities has enabled the Port of Hampton Roads to become a major destination for container ships.

CHAPTER THREE

THE GLOBAL CONNECTION

Trade—the act of buying, selling, or exchanging goods—can occur on a variety of different levels. A basic form of trade occurs between individuals, while a more complex version of trade exists within and among nations. The purpose of trade is to enable people to obtain items that they could not otherwise procure.

International trade, which is the exchange of goods between nations, has existed for thousands of years. African, Arabian, and Asian caravans (large groups of traders traveling together) are examples of early trade among empires. Many European rulers of the Middle Ages

Mountains of coal await shipment at the Pier IX Terminal in Newport News (facing page). *The terminal can accommodate vessels up to 1,000 feet long.*

49

saw the Crusades—religious wars between Christians and Muslims—as an opportunity to establish lucrative trade routes to the Middle East. In the 1400s and 1500s, European explorers such as Christopher Columbus and Juan Ponce de Léon visited North America, and trade with Native Americans resulted. By the 1600s, European countries were conducting trade with their colonies in North America.

Through trade, nations enjoy a greater variety and a larger quantity of goods. Most nations specialize in the manufacture and export of items they can produce cheaply. The money earned from selling these items enables nations to import goods they want or need. In general, imported goods are either manufactured items that have been produced more efficiently in other countries or they are raw materials, such as coal or grain, that importing nations don't have. When a country sells more items than it buys, that country is earning more money from trade than it is spending. This creates a positive **balance of trade.** When a country buys more than it sells, the country has a negative balance of trade.

➤ Because modern cargo vessels can carry huge quantities, waterborne shipping is the principal means of world transportation.

➤ In 1995 the Port of Hampton Roads earned more than $36 million dollars through foreign trade.

◄ Cargoes and Trading Partners

The first important trade commodity for the Virginia colony was tobacco, which was exported to Europe beginning in the 1600s. In the 1990s, in addition to tobacco, Norfolk and the other ports of Hampton Roads export and import a wide variety of goods to and from more than 100 countries. In the mid-1990's more than 51 million tons of cargo passed through the Port of Hampton Roads. Bulk cargo makes up the majority of this tonnage, but over the past few years the port has seen growth in the movement of **general cargo,** which includes breakbulk commodities and container cargo.

Export business is a major source of the shipping activity in Norfolk. In fact, exports account for almost 80 percent of all Hampton Roads trade. Italy has been the port's leading export partner, receiving more than 7 million tons of cargo. More than 5 million tons of cargo travel to the Netherlands and Japan, while France, Brazil, and Belgium each receive more than 3 million tons. Other export partners include Britain, South Korea, Turkey, and Egypt.

The port's largest export item is coal—a dry bulk cargo that is shipped to more than 20 countries—with Italy, the Netherlands, and Japan topping the list. The nations that import coal depend on the mineral to provide fuel for homes and factories. Coal-handling facilities in Norfolk and Newport News together ship more coal for export and coastal distribution than any other port in the United States. At more than 700,000

A 1.5-mile-long train (above), *carrying coal from the mines of western Virginia, heads to the port and to a waiting ship* (right).

FROM COAL TO CARS

Miners extract coal, the port's number-one export, from hundreds of locations in western Virginia and in West Virginia. Workers load the coal onto **hopper cars,** which carry the mineral by rail directly to terminals at Norfolk Southern Pier Six. Two side-by-side traveling loaders dump four hopper cars onto two conveyor belt systems. Coal is then fed to the loaders and onto coal ships, called colliers, at a rate of 5,000 tons per hour. Twin surge silos provide short-term storage and enable coal to be continually dumped while shiploaders are being repositioned for hold and vessel changes.

Automated dumping allows the blending and mixing of different types of coal originating from as many as 130 coal mines. The advantage to blending and mixing is that the port can provide its customers with their specific needs of coal.

After a collier is loaded, it sets sail for one of the many foreign ports, like Genoa, Italy, that import coal from Norfolk. After the collier arrives at Genoa, workers transfer the coal from the collier to hopper cars that carry the fuel to one of Italy's steel plants, where it will be used to provide energy for the production of steel. The finished steel is sent to factories that make machinery, including automobiles, power tools, and motor scooters. Some of this machinery is then shipped back to the United States through Norfolk and other U.S. ports.

An automated ship loader feeds grain into the holds of a cargo vessel. The port ships wheat, barley, and other grains to ports around the world.

tons, unmilled wheat is the port's second leading bulk export. Other bulk exports include barley, animal feed, iron waste and scrap metal, and oil seeds.

While coal exports remain vital to the Port of Hampton Roads, general cargo exports are becoming increasingly important. Pulp and waste paper, shipped in containers and used to make paper products, rank highest among general cargo export items. Wood pulp comes to Norfolk by train and truck from lumber companies throughout the northeastern United States, while waste paper arrives at the port from just about every part of the country. In 1995 the port exported more than 670,000 tons of each of these items. Other major container exports are auto parts and poultry—one of Virginia's leading agricultural products. More than 100,000 tons each of tobacco and tobacco products are exported annually. Logs and lumber are the leading breakbulk exports.

On the import side, more than 9 million tons of goods are imported through the port of Hampton Roads each year. The leading import

The port can handle a variety of import cargoes, including breakbulk commodities such as steel (left), *which is shipped in large coils, and cacao beans* (below), *which arrive in sacks.*

partners are Venezuela, Colombia, Greece, Britain, Germany, Brazil, and France. Crude (unrefined) oil, a liquid bulk cargo, leads the list of major imports for the area, with more than 3 million tons imported annually. Refined oil ranks next with approximately 840,000 tons. Special ships called tankers bring the crude oil and other liquid commodities to Hampton Roads, where it is piped into storage tanks. Some of these vessels weigh more than 200,000 tons. Many tankers are equipped with environmental safeguards to protect against spills and leakage.

Natural rubber, the top general cargo import, comes to Hampton Roads from Malaysia. In the mid-1990's the port received more than 290,000 tons of this commodity, which is used to create such items as tires and hoses. Paper and paperboard has been a large import item since 1995, when Stora, the third largest paper company in the world, began importing newsprint from

Sweden and Germany. Iron and steel, aluminum, and cacao beans are leading breakbulk imports. Lime and cement, stone, sand, and gravel are major dry bulk imports. The Nissan automobile company, based in Japan, imports 25,000 cars each year through Newport News Marine Terminal.

These days container traffic dominates growth at the port. Of the 9.7 million tons of general cargo moved through the port in 1996, more than 9 million tons was in container cargo. This is consistent with international trends, as more than 90 percent of the world's general cargo is currently transported in containers. Containerization saves shippers money, because container ships can be loaded more quickly than breakbulk cargo vessels. As a result, Hampton Roads has recently seen a decline in the movement of breakbulk commodities.

Worldwide > More than 75 shipping lines travel to Norfolk
Shipping Routes from all over the globe. These commercial carriers follow several major shipping routes to transport goods. A number of factors determine the route a ship takes. Passages between North America and Europe usually go directly across the Atlantic Ocean. At certain times of the year, however, ships crossing the Atlantic divert southward to avoid icebergs drifting from the Arctic Ocean. Shipping companies prefer direct routes, which save time, fuel, and money.

One of the most heavily used paths is the North Atlantic route, which connects North America to markets in northern Europe. Ships carrying cargo from the Netherlands or Britain, for example, might follow this route to Norfolk.

Another busy shipping passage is the South American route, which sees traffic from both U.S. coasts and from Canada. A ship carrying cargo to Norfolk from Venezuela or Brazil would follow this route. The last major passage is the Mediterranean-Asiatic-Australasian route, which extends eastward through the Mediterranean Sea and the Indian Ocean to Asia and Australia.

The U.S. Customs Service, located in Norfolk, plays an important role in monitoring trade and shipping activity within the port. When an international cargo ship arrives at the port, the ship's agent must report to the customhouse and make an official entry of the vessel. Cargo cannot be unloaded before formal entry is made. Customs officers oversee this process and collect tonnage taxes and user fees, which are charged on all international cargo ships entering the port. The Customs Service is also responsible for

➤ Ships moving through Hampton Roads travel to more than 250 ports in 100 different countries.

➤ Goods imported into the United States via Hampton Roads end up in many markets throughout the country, including Miami, Kansas City, and New Orleans.

Norfolk welcomes ships from all over the world, like this container vessel from Keelung, a port in Taiwan.

combating smuggling operations. For example, narcotics traffickers sometimes try to smuggle illegal drugs into the United States on cargo ships. U.S. Customs officers at Norfolk are working with shipping lines to prevent this problem.

Economic Systems ➤ Economic systems throughout the world vary and handle trade in different ways. In a centrally planned economy, such as the one in China, private ownership of industries, businesses, and resources is usually limited. The government sets economic goals, directs the processes of production, and makes trade decisions. Countries operating under this type of economic system aim for self-sufficiency and the ability to produce all the goods necessary for their citizens. Free enterprise, on the other hand, is a system in which production of goods is privately operated. In this kind of system, private persons and businesses, rather than the government, respond to consumer needs and are responsible for the shipment and distribution of goods.

International trade within the free-enterprise system involves a number of players. While shipping lines physically move cargo to and from Norfolk and other ports, freight forwarding companies help exporters and importers arrange this movement of goods. If a company needs help sending a product overseas, it will provide the freight forwarder with a complete description of the goods and how they are packaged. The freight forwarder then finds a suitable shipping line, books passage for the cargo, and gives the exporting company the shipping schedule. If necessary, the freight forwarder provides intermodal transportation from the customer to the port. When companies want to import foreign goods, freight forwarders act as customs brokers, preparing all paperwork for U.S. Customs and paying duties. Brokers also make sure that import cargo is released by the shipping line and delivered to the importer. More than 20 freight forwarding companies are located in Norfolk, helping transport a variety of items in and out of the port.

Wholesalers and retailers are important links in the import chain. Wholesalers buy large quantities of goods directly from the producer or importer. In addition, wholesalers may also provide storage locations, arrange for delivery, develop sales promotions, conduct market research, and take care of billing and collections. After purchasing the goods, the wholesaler then sells them to a retailer, who is the direct link between producers and consumers. Several types of retailers exist in Norfolk and around the country. Store retailers operate supermarkets, department stores, and restaurants. Non-store retailers include door-to-door salespeople, vending machines, and mail-order businesses. Examples of service retailing are gas stations, catering services, and dry-cleaning services.

> Goods such as coffee, grain, cotton, sugar, and metals are sometimes sold in an organized open market. At this market, called a commodity exchange, prices are determined by market supply and demand.

Trade Regulations

Numerous worldwide regulations direct domestic and international trade. The most common type of regulation is the **tariff,** a tax usually placed on imports. The purpose of a tariff is to discourage consumers from buying an imported item, thereby protecting a domestic manufacturer that produces a similar item.

Consumers are generally attracted to the locally made item because it is cheaper than the taxed import. Another kind of trade restriction is the **quota,** a limit on the amount of imports of a specific good that a nation will accept. As with tariffs, governments use quotas to protect their own industries from foreign competition. Developing nations will often impose quotas on specific goods to protect newly operating industries in their country. Governments sometimes impose export quotas to conserve raw materials in short supply.

At the Port of Hampton Roads, cotton from India and peanuts from Brazil are limited by quotas to protect the U.S. cotton and peanut industries. After quotas on these commodities have been filled, port officials cannot allow them to be shipped to the importer. Cargo that exceeds a quota is stored at warehouses in Norfolk that are monitored by U.S. Customs officers. The goods remain in the warehouses until the yearly quota opens up, at which point they can be shipped to the importing company.

Tariffs and quotas are both forms of **protectionism**—the practice of shielding a country's industries from foreign competition. Many economists believe that such restrictions cause more harm than good. By safeguarding inefficient industries, protectionist policies limit more productive uses of a country's resources. Poor countries may also suffer from weakened economies if their exports are limited.

Trade Agreements ➤ Many countries have signed trade agreements to remove tariffs and other trade regulations. One example is the European Union, which

was created in 1958. The member-countries of this community have formed a free-trade area in which goods and services move across European national boundaries without restrictions or tariffs. In 1989 Canada and the United States signed a free-trade pact that laid the groundwork for the North American Free Trade Agreement (NAFTA), which went into effect January 1, 1994. NAFTA provides for the removal of all barriers to trade in goods and services between the United States, Canada, and Mexico. According to this agreement, advertising and trucking restrictions were lifted immediately. Limits on banking and insurance-company ownership as well as tariffs on farm products,

With Vice President Al Gore and congressional leaders looking on, U.S. president Bill Clinton signs the North American Free Trade Agreement (NAFTA).

U.S. cars, and approximately 10,000 other commodities will be eliminated gradually. The U.S. government hopes that NAFTA will create more trade with Mexico, resulting in more business for Norfolk and other U.S. ports.

International trade changes over time as the demand for products and services grows in some areas and decreases in others. To stay on top of the shifts in international trade, the Virginia Port Authority maintains marketing and sales departments in Belgium, Brazil, South Korea, and Singapore. Port officials at these branches work to promote the port as an ideal shipping location for foreign businesses. These efforts will help keep imports and exports flowing through Norfolk for years to come.

Marketing efforts by the Virginia Port Authority should keep port terminals busy for many years.

CHAPTER FOUR

THE PORT AND THE CITY

The past and the present come together everyday in Hampton Roads. The **American Rover** *(facing page) is a graceful sailing ship that takes visitors on two- and three-hour tours of the harbor.*

Visitors and newcomers to Virginia are often confused by all the terms that describe Norfolk and the surrounding area. It's referred to as Southeastern Virginia, Tidewater, Hampton Roads, and Greater Norfolk. In addition, the names of individual cities and counties in the Norfolk area are commonly used.

Norfolk is one of nine cities and five counties that make up what is most correctly called Hampton Roads. Since 1990 all the region's mail has been postmarked with Hampton Roads instead of with individual city or county names. Although the cities and counties of

Hampton Roads have much in common, each maintains its own flavor. With a population of just over 266,000, Norfolk is the second largest city in Hampton Roads. As the nucleus of the Hampton Roads area, Norfolk serves as a center for distribution, trade, financial activities, the arts, and vacationing.

For nearly 400 years, the naturally deep waters of Hampton Roads have played a vital role in the development of Norfolk as the region's hub. Within a two-block radius are the regional headquarters for all the major banks in the state of Virginia. Norfolk Southern Corporation, whose railroads travel through 20 states and Canada, is headquartered in downtown Norfolk as well. United Services Automobile Association has a corporate complex in Norfolk. The city also serves as the cultural center of the Hampton Roads area. Residents can listen to the Virginia Symphony, watch a production of the Virginia Stage Company, attend the Virginia Opera, visit the Chrysler Museum of Art, or participate in numerous smaller art groups.

➤ Norfolk's climate is considered one of the most desirable by the National Weather Service. Norfolk is located north of the usual track of hurricanes, and south of the normal path of winter storms.

➤ Norfolk's sister cities include Norfolk County, England; Wilhelmshaven, Germany; Toulon, France; Kitakyushu, Japan; and Kaliningrad, Russia.

The Chrysler Museum of Art houses more than 30,000 objects, including works from African, Islamic, and Asian cultures.

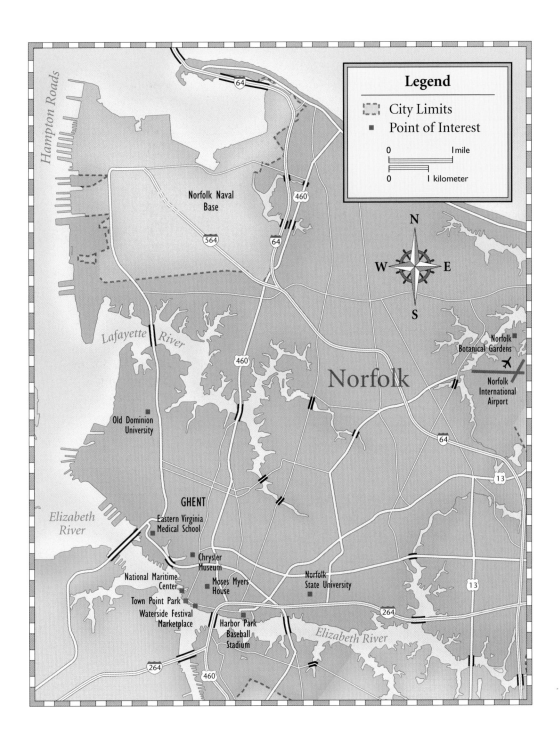

Legend

[ ] City Limits

■ Point of Interest

0　　　　　1 mile

0　　　　1 kilometer

N
W　　E
S

Hampton Roads

Norfolk Naval Base

Lafayette River

Old Dominion University

Elizabeth River

GHENT

Eastern Virginia Medical School

Chrysler Museum

National Maritime Center

Moses Myers House

Town Point Park

Waterside Festival Marketplace

Harbor Park Baseball Stadium

Norfolk State University

Norfolk

Norfolk Botanical Gardens

Norfolk International Airport

Elizabeth River

The Waterside Festival Marketplace (left) *and Nauticus* (above) *are two of downtown Norfolk's most popular attractions. The Waterside has more than 100 shops, restaurants, and nightclubs, while Nauticus offers virtual reality flight simulators and other kinds of interactive exhibits.*

Downtown Norfolk ➤ Waterfront cities often clutter their shorelines with high-rise buildings and other construction, blocking a view of the water. Norfolk has managed its harbor development to enable residents and visitors to enjoy scenic vistas of the Elizabeth River and the Chesapeake Bay. The Waterside, a waterfront marketplace of shops and restaurants, has revitalized downtown Norfolk. Built in 1983, this large complex replaced decaying warehouses. In 1993 Harbor Park baseball stadium, also on the waterfront, opened as home of the Triple A Norfolk Tides, the farm team of the New York Mets. The National Maritime Center (Nauticus)—a high-tech educational and entertainment complex that highlights marine exploration, navigation, shipbuilding, and ocean research—opened in downtown Norfolk in 1994.

Also located in the downtown area are a few of Norfolk's historic homes and neighborhoods. The Moses Myers House, home of Norfolk's first permanent Jewish settler, is the only historic house in the United States interpreting the traditions of early Jewish residents. Ghent is a neighborhood of cafes, museums, boutiques and turn-of-the-century homes where doctors and lawyers mix with artists and college students.

Norfolk offers a variety of attractions to visitors and tourists. The large number of beaches throughout the area are popular attractions. Other places of interest include Norfolk Botanical Gardens and Norfolk Naval Base, where visitors can tour selected ships on the weekends. The region is also rich in colonial history. Within the Hampton Roads area, tourists can travel to

➤ Attractions at Nauticus include a multimedia naval battle show, a shark-petting tank, and a 600-foot pier that hosts tours of naval and commercial vessels.

➤ More than 4 million people visit Hampton Roads each year, making tourism a $1.5 million industry employing more than 40,000 workers.

During Harborfest, a celebration of Norfolk's maritime heritage, visitors and residents alike can tour historic ships docked along Town Point Park.

Colonial Williamsburg, the Jamestown Settlement, and Yorktown Battlefield—site of the last battle of the American Revolution.

Throughout the year, Norfolk hosts numerous free festivals, many of which are held on the waterfront at Town Point Park. In June the park is the site of Harborfest, an annual celebration of Norfolk's maritime heritage, featuring historic ships, nautical races, and fireworks. The International Azalea Festival, which honors Norfolk's role as headquarters for NATO's Supreme Allied Commander Atlantic, is held at the Norfolk Botanical Gardens. Each year this event pays tribute to a different NATO member-nation with an array of cultural, athletic, trade, and social events.

Norfolk is also a center for higher education, with campuses for Old Dominion University, Virginia Wesleyan College, Norfolk State University, and Eastern Virginia Medical

➤ Town Point Park is a great spot to watch the parade of commercial, naval, and personal vessels that sail through the port each day.

School, where the first test-tube baby in the United States was conceived in 1981.

Population ➤ The population of Norfolk and the Hampton Roads area is a diverse mix of cultures and nationalities. The African-American community makes up more than 40 percent of Norfolk's population. There is also a significant Asian community, represented by people from Japan, South Korea, China, Thailand, Cambodia, the Philippines, and Laos. Other ethnic groups include Native Americans and people from Latin America. An Islamic cultural center, located in Norfolk, is a meeting place for Muslims who live in the Hampton Roads area. In addition, foreign military officers come to live in Norfolk and other Hampton Roads cities while serving on the NATO staff.

A distinctive feature of Norfolk is its significant military population. Seven of the country's largest military installations are located in Hampton Roads. As a result, the Norfolk metropolitan area has one of the largest concentrations of military activity in the nation. There are more than 95,000 active duty U.S. Navy and Marine Corps personnel at Norfolk Naval Base.

But the presence of the military also causes a sizable turnover in Norfolk's population as military personnel move in and out. The Hampton Roads region ranks second to Orlando, Florida, in the mobility of its population. Yet it's not uncommon for military personnel to have been stationed in the Norfolk area at one time and then to return permanently after retirement. An estimated 44,000 military retirees make their homes in Hampton Roads.

The presence of the naval base makes Norfolk a popular residence for military personnel.

Norfolk and the area's other ports drive the Hampton Roads economy. The Port of Hampton Roads generates more than 116,000 jobs, $323 million in tax revenues, and $3 billion in wages. Many of the jobs directly related to the port involve the physical movement of goods. Pilots guide cargo ships through the Norfolk Channel, dockworkers load and unload cargo, and railroad employees help move cargo in and out of the port. Other jobs include the operation of terminals and warehouses, the maintenance of containers, the weighing and sampling of cargo, and the servicing of cranes and other port equipment.

These various jobs form only part of the area's large service industry, which employs more than 86 percent of the labor force in the Hampton Roads region. The service industry includes jobs in transportation, communications, government, education, real estate, retail sales, and tourism. The service industry is growing steadily in areas not related to the port. Numerous companies employ thousands of people to process credit card transactions, to take orders for merchandise, to handle insurance claims, and to do telemarketing. These are sometimes referred to as fulfillment industries.

Manufacturing is also a significant part of the economy, with shipbuilding and repair at the top of the list. A total of 20 shipyards design, build, overhaul, and repair all kinds of commercial and military ships. Norfolk is home to the Norfolk Shipbuilding and Drydock Corporation (NORSHIPCO). The world's largest shipyard, Newport News Shipbuilding, is located just across the Hampton Roads waterway in

Workers repair a military vessel in one of Norfolk's dry docks. Shipbuilding and repair is a leading industry in the Hampton Roads area.

Newport News, Virginia. Shipyards in the area employ more than 30,000 people.

For many years, the economy of the area relied on the military, the port, and tourism. But more than 125 internationally based companies have set up operations in the Hampton Roads region. Examples of a few of the larger firms are Canon Virginia (Japan), which manufactures copiers; Stihl Inc. (Germany), which makes chainsaws; and Volvo Penta Production, Inc. (Sweden), which produces marine engines. Major U.S. manufacturers in Norfolk include the Ford Motor Company, whose Norfolk assembly plant produces pickup trucks and employs more than 2,000 people.

Despite downsizing, the military is still an economic force in the area. In the mid-1990's, the military employed more than 162,000 enlisted personnel and civilians. The navy alone brings more than $10 billion into the region, and the naval base is Norfolk's largest employer.

Hampton Roads is also the third most productive fishing region in the country. The area yields an annual haul of 103 million pounds of oysters, clams, crabs, and finfish. The Chesapeake Bay's blue crab harvest accounts for more than half the country's total annual catch. Numerous processing plants in the area help move seafood from the water to retail and wholesale markets. Norfolk's restaurants are famous for their excellent seafood dishes.

A fishing boat brings in the day's catch.

For any port to operate successfully, it needs a strong, flexible workforce. The most advantageous location in the world won't bring a port business if the cost of labor is too high, or if frequent labor disputes interrupt service. Because of the strong relationship between the labor force and port managers, the International Longshoremen's Association (ILA) classifies

◄ Port Labor and Management

Hampton Roads as a "labor-model port." Norfolk and the other ports have not experienced a locally based labor strike since the early 1980s. Cooperation between labor and management has proved to be an advantage that port customers appreciate.

The ILA works to protect port laborers and wages. Working together, the ILA and port management have created an apprentice program to help keep labor costs down. Under the

A solid relationship between port workers and management has prevented strikes and has improved the port's efficiency.

A tugboat heads towards the Chesapeake Bay to meet an incoming vessel. At the Port of Hampton Roads, shipping and trade go on 24 hours a day.

apprentice program, newly hired dockworkers earn a lower wage handling only breakbulk goods. After a period of time, the apprentices start handling containers, where wage rates are higher. The apprentice program provides the port with a labor force that can compete with other regional ports. This agreement between labor and management—the first of its kind in the U.S. port industry—plays an important role in attracting new shipping lines to Hampton Roads.

Norfolk and the other Hampton Roads ports have relatively theft-free cargo terminals. Many ports lose millions of dollars in stolen cargo each year. At the Port of Hampton Roads less than 1 percent of the total cargo shipped through the port is lost to theft. Port officials credit the well-trained, 71-person port police department for keeping theft figures low.

Port police are also involved with ensuring port safety. A port terminal can be a dangerous place. Tall equipment such as cranes move heavy loads high above the docks. Trucks and trains come right into the terminal buildings. Port police attend all safety meetings to learn about what goes on at the port and what safety measures workers should take to avoid unnecessary accidents.

A satisfied workforce and a safe port will keep shipping lines coming back to Norfolk in the future. In addition, planned expansion of port facilities will attract new customers. Norfolk has always been a gateway for shipping and trade. From the earliest tobacco ships to the container ships of the present, Norfolk has hosted vessels from all over the world. As a hub of military operations, Norfolk has helped defend the country. The port and the city have seen hard times in the past, but the future looks bright.

GLOSSARY

balance of trade: The difference over time between the value of a country's imports and its exports.

ballast tank: A hold, or tank, deep within a ship that is filled with water or other heavy substances to keep the vessel stable.

breakbulk cargo: A term used to refer to non-containerized general cargo. This cargo category includes items packaged in separate units, such as boxes, cases, and pallets, as well as heavy machinery that is too big to be transported in a container.

bulk cargo: Raw products, such as grains and minerals, that are not packaged in separate units. Dry bulk cargo is typically piled loosely in a ship's cargo holds, while liquid bulk cargo is piped into a vessel's storage tanks.

chandler: A dealer who sells supplies or equipment of a certain kind.

dredging: The process of digging up and removing sediment from the bed of a waterway. Dredging deepens the waterway and creates a stockpile of earth that can be used as a landfill elsewhere.

dry dock: A dock where a vessel is kept out of the water so that repairs can be made to the parts that lie below the water line.

gantry crane: A crane mounted on a platform supported by a framed structure. The crane runs on parallel tracks so it can span or rise above a ship to load and unload heavy cargo.

general cargo: Cargo that is not shipped in bulk. This cargo category includes containerized and breakbulk cargo.

hopper car: A freight car with a floor that slants downward toward a hinged door, which swings open to release bulk cargo.

intermodal transportation:
A system of transportation in which goods are moved from one type of vehicle to another, such as from a ship to a train or from a train to a truck, in the course of a single trip.

protectionism: A trade philosophy of protecting a nation's economy by controlling trade with other countries. Countries that protect their markets often allow only certain types of goods into their country.

quota: A limit on the amount of imports and exports of specific goods a nation will accept.

tariff: A tax on imported goods. A specific tariff is applied to each unit of an imported good. An ad-valorem tariff is a tax charged to the importer as a percentage of the price of the good.

TEU: Twenty-foot equivalent unit. Container traffic is measured in TEUs. One TEU represents a container that is 20 feet long, 8 feet wide, and 8.5 or 9.5 feet high.

PRONUNCIATION GUIDE

Algonquian	al-GAHN-kwee-uhn
Chesapeake	CHEHS-uh-PEEK
Chickahominy	CHIH-kah-hahm-mih-NEE
Kiskiack	Kih-SKEE-ack
Kecoughtan	KICK-uh-tan
Nansemond	NANS-muhnd
Norfolk	NOR-fohk
Powhatan	pow-uh-TAN
Susquehannock	suhs-kwuh-HAHN-ok
Tockwogh	TAHK-wuh

INDEX

METRIC CONVERSION CHART

WHEN YOU KNOW	MULTIPLY BY	TO FIND
inches	2.54	centimeters
feet	0.3048	meters
miles	1.609	kilometers
square feet	0.0929	square meters
square miles	2.59	square kilometers
acres	0.4047	hectares
pounds	0.454	kilograms
tons	0.9072	metric tons
bushels	0.0352	cubic meters
gallons	3.7854	liters

ABOUT THE AUTHOR

Linda Wirkner is a former elementary school teacher and historical interpreter for the Colonial Williamsburg Foundation. She is the author of *Mystery of the Blue-Gowned Ghost* and has also written more than 100 articles and stories for children's magazines. *Destination Norfolk* is her first book for the Lerner Publishing Group. Ms. Wirkner lives with her husband in Yorktown, Virginia.

ACKNOWLEDGMENTS

The author would like to express her appreciation to the following people, organizations, and companies for providing information and resources: Linda Ford, Public Relations Department, Virginia Port Authority; Joseph Dorto, President of Norfolk International Terminal; Bill Brown, Public Affairs Officer, U.S. Army Corps of Engineers, Norfolk District; Virginia Pilot Association; Hampton Roads Maritime Association; Virginia Tourism Corporation, Virginia International Terminals; Norfolk Convention and Visitors Bureau; Cargill, Inc.; ASL Travel, Yorktown, VA; City of Norfolk Home Page; Virginia Department of Economic Development, Richmond, VA; Hampton Roads Central Library; and the *Virginian-Pilot*.